U0131397

赤裸的心

蔣友梅

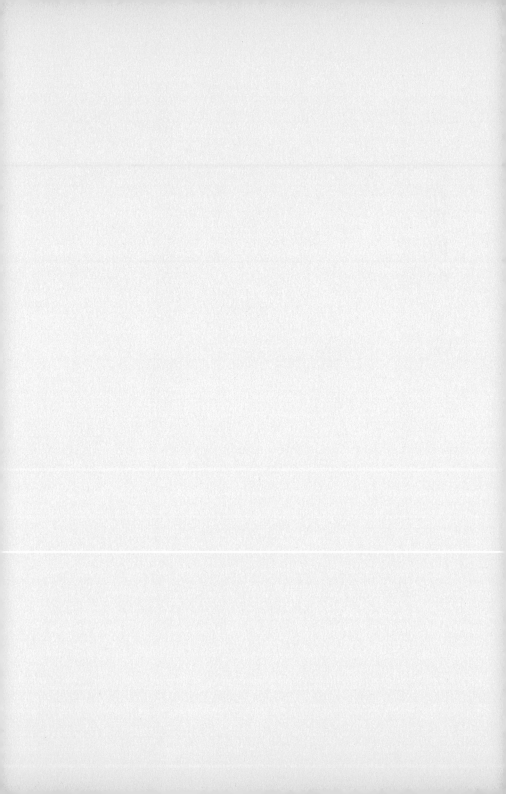

—

For my daughter Zoë,
who taught me how to live.

—

自序

紙和筆是我最老的朋友。小時候比較孤單，習慣觀察周遭環境，寫故事、畫圖也就成了生活的一部分。在線條、文字和意象中，找到了一塊完全屬於自己的空間。現實和想像之間的界線是主觀、模糊的，穿遊其間的是意象。對我來說，視覺藝術創作是詩意象的延伸，本來就是一體的。二〇一三年出版第一本詩集《浮生記行》的構想是想做出一系列 artist's books，以自己的攝影作為設計主軸，希望文字和圖像節奏共鳴，發出一個完整的聲音。

二〇一四年有一個機緣拜訪佛教王國不丹。帶著香客的心，踏尋蓮花生大師千百年前留下的足跡，反璞歸真，深受感動。第二本詩集《赤裸的心》由此而起。

目次

自序	05
古道	12
仲夏日	13
心傳	16
蓮師洞（一）	20
蓮師洞（二）	21
曾經你的腳步	24
無我	27
化空	29
妳蒼黃的髮絲	32

破碎的天　　　　　　　　34

昨夜夢到一場雨　　　　36

點燈　　　　　　　　　40

生命　　　　　　　　　43

六歲的馬可斯說　　　　44

心供　　　　　　　　　47

喇嘛　　　　　　　　　49

奇緣　　　　　　　　　52

你走了　　　　　　　　55

蓮師洞（三）　　　　　57

月圓時　　　　　　　　60

靜　　　　　　　　　　63

金蟬主宰大地時　　　　64

獻給無名的死者　　　　68

赤裸的婚禮　　　　　　71

老樹　　　　　　　　　73

火湖　　　　　　　　　75

破碎　　　　　　　　　78

藍調　　　　　　　　　80

古道

這青苔密布的石階
是一冊被遺忘的古經
無意中
被出沒無常的光影
揭露了

看到了
前塵香客的足跡
也感覺到
萬古千秋數珠默誦的應和

蜿蜒的古道
是蓮師的手印
被驚醒的
是我的足聲

仲夏日

沉悶的仲夏日
一道銀光劃破黑天
意外的序曲
揭開了嶄新的樂章

破碎的天
也訝異
不知什麼時候
吐出絲絲金沫
點亮了大地

輓詩中的歡樂頌

沉悶的仲夏日
鬆口氣
輕了腳步
翩然起舞

不知不覺中
天
已呈一片淡青灰

心傳

久別了
滿面風塵的行客
終究歸根

百年前供的香火
餘香猶存

路邊
一隻瘸腳的流浪狗
無意回眸

似曾相識的眼神
也是恩師的傳承

千山萬水
原來
未曾告別

蓮師洞（一）

風雨是大悲咒
岩洞的建築師

我的眼淚
是一串串剛出水的海珠

趺坐在蓮師洞裡
如夢初覺
一無雜念

布姆唐山谷（Bumthang Valley）

布姆唐山谷是不丹東部的佛教聖地。在不丹王國統一前，布姆唐曾經是一個小王國。據說西元八世紀，布姆唐辛度國王（Sindhu Raja）被魔鬼附身，從印度請蓮花生大師來祛邪。祛邪成功後，布姆唐成為佛教王國。布姆唐山谷仍保存著蓮師當年閉關的山洞，俗稱「蓮師洞」。

蓮師洞（二）

佛陀的面容
在燭光下
微微顫抖
忽隱忽滅
在心中
卻清晰如舊

這石窟
是神話的遺骸
無言的見證

一片寧靜
只有原音
在天地間迴響
山林草木
皆是大自然的手印
大地的情歌
看它們
仰天迎接
宇宙無量的恩賜

曾經你的腳步

赤足的你
腳跡是金的
腳掌卻血漬斑斑

瘡口就是癒合了
還是瘡口

你的血
也是大地的血
乾了還是血

他們說
有一天
你的血
會變成金光
來無影
去無蹤

無我

六月在布姆唐山谷
一隻金鷹
展翅凌空

吹起了心的翅膀
吹散了恐懼的網
徐來一陣清風

我
開暢的心
隨著金鷹
騰雲駕霧

化空

思維頭緒
難以捉摸
像一再漏網的通緝犯

思維本質
終究無質
一鬆手
就化空

緊抓著
就成了逃犯的奴隸
恐懼的奴隸
期盼的奴隸

妳蒼黃的髮絲

冬一揮手
解開了殘月蒼黃的髮髻
慰撫寂寞的夜

雖然
已經淡忘了妳的五官
但我還是記得妳的金熒
無言的
反映深夜的赤裸

妳
纖細蒼黃的髮絲
勾起了一個遠古的記憶
不知不覺間
我也金光閃爍
脫胎黑夜的女神
卸下一層垂死的星辰

破碎的天

大地是一片破碎的天
墜星
依依不捨
耿耿思源

皎月
不禁淚下
哭出忘洋記川
洗滌千年不癒的瘡口

怎忘得了曾經
懸浮在吐納間
天地本是同一場夢

昨夜夢到
一場雨

昨夜夢到一場雨
沖破血紅的天
洗淨世間一切汙漬

洶湧澎湃的雨
毫不留情

天的血淚
穿透頂輪
灌滿了全身

夢中
看見自己
頭頂
懸浮著一條銜尾蛇
神祕的火輪
喚醒了沉默千年的魔咒

金光已染透半邊天

銜尾蛇

在神話中常見的銜尾蛇（Ouroboros）是一個自古流傳的符號，大致形象為一條蛇（或龍）正在唔食自己的尾巴，形成一個圓環。這個符號有許多不同的象徵意義：最被人接受的是「無限」、「循環」、「再生」等。銜尾蛇在煉金術中更是重要的徵記。心理學家榮格（Jung）認為它反映了人類心理的原型。

點燈

順風
朋友
願妳坦然無畏
渡到彼岸

讓這盞燈
照亮妳的回程

願妳
輕輕鬆鬆解開
柔情的枷鎖

平安歸去

點燈

作者在不丹古杰寺接到朋友過世的消息，爲她和留世的先生、四歲的小女兒點燈。

生命

從呱呱墜地的那一刻
死亡
就像一塊隱形的裹屍布
輕輕纏住我們

時間
吐出一絲絲恐懼和希望
越織越密
越縛越緊
直到有一天
動彈不得

懷念最初的蠶繭
耐心等待脫殼
迎接死亡的開始

六歲的馬可斯說

我是銀河勇士
披上燦爛的星夜
騎著千彩海馬
手揮水晶魔劍
凌空馳騁

「馬可斯，別做白日夢！」

我和海馬
瞬間墜地
無家可歸

好高興認識你
跟我一起來玩好不好
我來扮海天王
你要扮什麼隨你
在我的世界裡
沒有什麼不可以

馬可斯

馬可斯是一個六歲的小男孩；在哈伯島渡假時常找作者聊天。

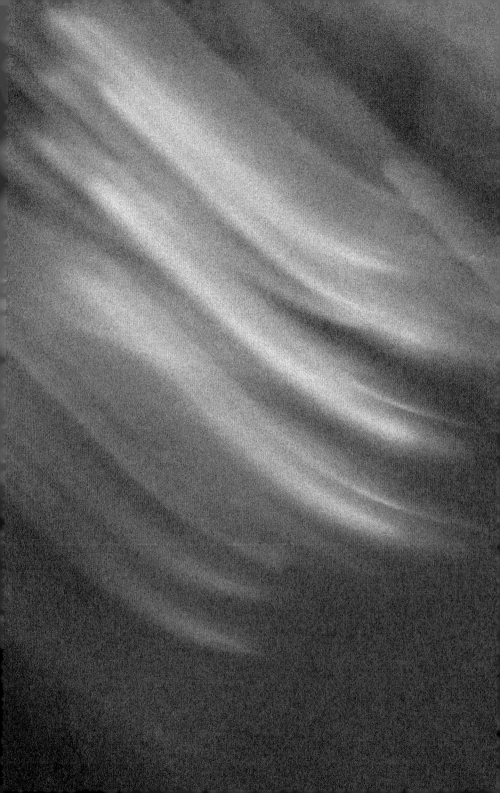

喇嘛

突來一陣晚風
吹散了夕陽的夢
大地
一霎間光芒萬丈

熒熒光波中一抹紅
是喇嘛
還是幻象

已經成為記憶
一時的燦爛
黃昏披上了夜空
天色漸漸轉暗

喇嘛的餘影
點燃了我蒼涼的心

喇嘛

藏傳佛教中，「喇嘛」是上師的尊稱。

心供

水磨對經輪潺潺細語
藉著風賜福

流浪狗的吠聲
是山上喇嘛誦經的回音

修得正見
供金供糞
都一樣

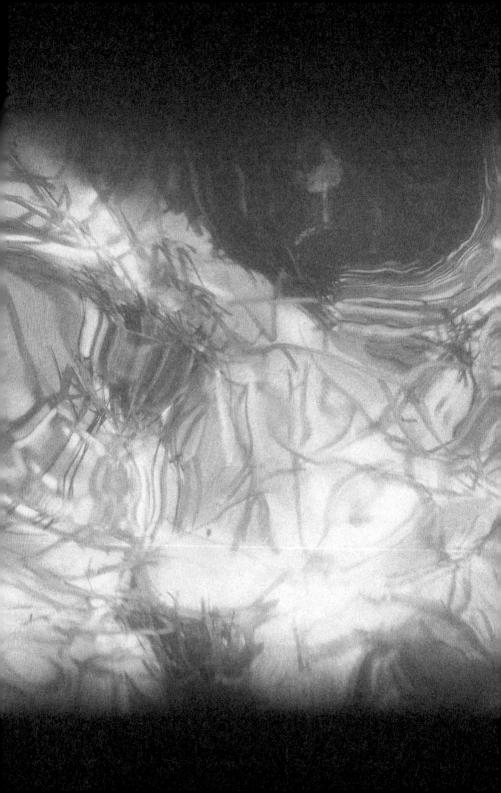

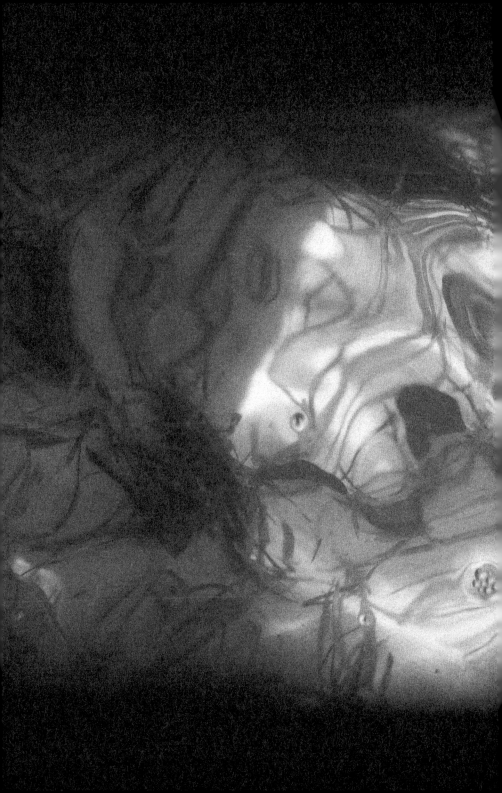

奇緣

地脈中流的
是龍的血
什麼時候
浸透了古寺殘壁

緩緩成形
在修行人息息吐納間
神話和薩滿的方外天地

一陣清風撲面
喚醒了長眠的心
玄妙的氣場
瀰漫十方

形影
幻現幻滅
出沒無常
一段奇緣
啊我赤裸的心

53

形影
幻現幻滅
出沒無常
一段奇緣
啊我赤裸的心

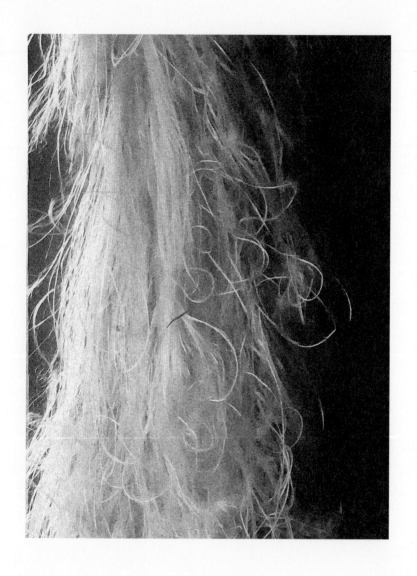

你走了

你走了

不曾爲你止步
四季晨昏
雨還是不停地下
還是繼續吹
風

我
仍舊天天起床
雖然夜夜難眠

你走了
越走越遠
我在夢中
無聲嘶喊

你的名字

你
帶走一切

無情地

蓮師洞（三）

老翁
盤坐在泥巴地上
從容不迫的
轉著經輪
低聲吟唱無言的心語
潺潺如水

一抹殘光
擦過他枯皺的臉
我
合掌致敬
他
以無牙的笑容回禮

經輪徐徐的轉
纏綿的韻律
像催眠曲

老翁　經輪和我
是懸在空中的同一首詩

遠處
時而
孤鐘鳴

老翁和經輪
已化為記憶
我
是夢
是醒

月圓時

多情的漁翁
從天宮
撒下一網晶瑩
點綴維納斯藍色的赤裸

初醒的海
仰天致謝
伸著懶腰
卸下層層夢影

滿懷私密的海
不再沉默
千萬隻記憶的手
打開時間的結
和夜空切切私語

溫柔的海
最原始的母親
低聲細語
頻頻召喚
喚起曾經
喚起我眷眷歸心

靜

靜
展開柔軟的雙臂
環抱一切
又回歸原點
自給自足
悠然自得

這份完美
多麼容易破碎

真傻：
思前思後
與其不如盡在其中

金蟬主宰
大地時

在這繁星綴空的夜晚
海風
傳來陣陣蟬鳴
喚起了原始的記憶

曾經
有一個不食煙火的時代
金蟬主宰大地的時代
沒有語言
也沒有思維
只有萬物心搏的應和

蟬告訴我
那曾是一個感知的世界

初音

千絲萬縷
連結萬象
天地一體

蟬聲愈來愈急促
好像急著提醒我
遺落的金蟬時代
不只是記憶

靜下心來
還是聽得到
遠古的回聲

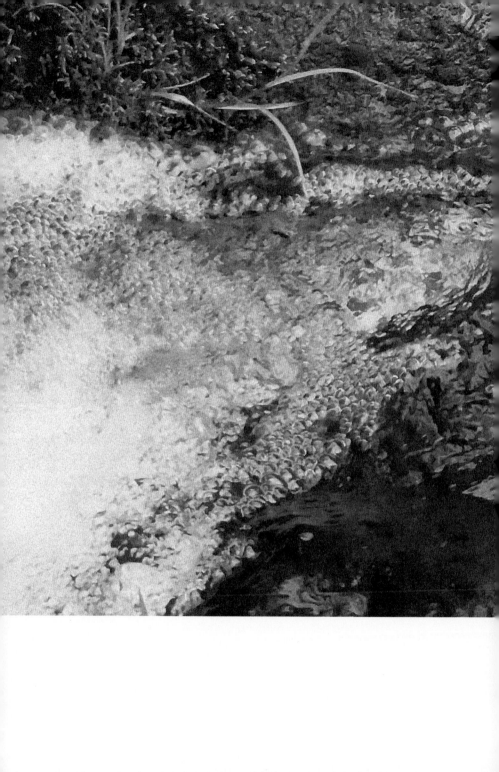

獻給無名的
死者

誰來悼念
被時間遺忘的遊魂
暴力的血祭
陽光的棄兒

隱隱綽綽的哀嚎
仍在空中迴響

多少無名的遺骸
早已腐爛
回歸塵土
成為歷史的廢墟

你可聽見

空洞的哭聲中
微搏的心脈
堅決守候著
鮮血的誓言

當所有的證人都不在
還剩下什麼

剩下的
是再隆重的謊言也遮不住的真理
時間是海
我們是浪
一心一體
不斷還魂

我的血肉是祭壇
和四季五行共同見證：
我們延續的
是同一個生命體

赤裸的
婚禮

七十年前的一場婚宴
結束在特雷布林卡
甜蜜的情歌
成了嗚咽的悲號

鬼故事中的亞當夏娃
給黑蟒的細語騙了
天真無邪的道別
赤裸的步向一個殘忍的未來
怎知
不會再有春天

枯黃的屍體
和一堆堆被遺棄的衣物

覆上一層層白霜，
像一座座冰山

這是他們唯一的遺書

飄零在空中的
是骨灰還是雪花

七十年後
故事還是沒有結局
人類的殘暴
到哪一個世紀才能化解

特雷布林卡

特雷布林卡（Treblinka）集中營是一個第二次世界大
戰時期納粹德國的滅絕營，位於波蘭，距離首都華沙約
一百公里的森林中。

老樹

仲夏：
老樹
溫柔地展開枝葉
給滋養它的土壤
遮蔭

反哺思源的老樹
很清楚自己的義務
毫無私心

什麼時候開始
人類成了大自然的凶手
自己的凶手
忘記了萬象本是同一個生命體

老樹
無言地
見證這一切

深秋：
它落淚了

等春天再來時
老樹
依舊趺坐原地
像佛陀
靜靜觀照一切

火湖

無名氏
解開纏綿身上的裹紗
徐徐坐起
淚盈盈的雙眼
清澄如鏡
赤裸的身軀
蒼白如月

瘡疤累累的腳下
是他破碎的紙冠
昔夢的墳堆

他走向神祕的火湖
心馳神往
湖面瀰漫著縷縷紅煙
無形的魔紗
像母親溫柔的懷抱

一剎那還是千萬年後他再現身
頭上戴著一頂熊熊火冠
一身金絲銀羽
如鏡的雙眼是雪亮的
無名氏
化成一片光芒
化解了茫茫思海
古今往來的千言萬語

火湖

「火在水中」的形象，在古今神話故事中相當普遍。例以北歐神話為題的華格納歌劇《尼伯龍根的指環》、托爾金的《魔戒之王》等名作中都出現「火在水中」的象徵符號。「火湖」一詩的靈感來源是布姆唐山谷中的火焰湖（Mebar Tsho）。傳說中不丹伏藏大師貝瑪·林巴（1450-1521）手持油燈潛入火焰湖，浮現時不但取得法寶，手中的油燈仍然火焰熊熊。

破碎

暖風吹散了樹影
破了夜的寧靜
雷雨聲
一絲你笑容的記憶
碎了我無辜的心

藍調

那天
電話中你說
好久不見
我們喝杯茶敘敘舊吧
你知道
今天是 Marcel Proust 的生日

有一兩年沒見了吧
聽藍調想到你
過得還好嗎

今天早上
他們告訴我
是愛滋病

今天
是 Marcel Proust 的生日
不知道
有沒有空
陪我聽聽藍調
喝杯茶

**every now
and then
a solitary bell**

by Chiang Yomei

———

For my daughter Zoë,
who taught me how to live.

———

This book was inspired by a
visit to the beautiful Buddhist
Kingdom of Bhutan.

CONTENT

PATH   12

HEART TEACHER   15

SHUG DRAK (1)   16

SHUG DRAK (2)   17

DISSOLUTION   19

SURRENDER   20

OFFERING   21

LAMP OFFERING   22

LAMA   24

SHUG DRAK (3)   27

LAND OF THE THUNDER DRAGON   28

UNSTRUCK SOUND   30

BLACK SKY IN SUMMER   31

AT THE FULL MOON   33

I DREAMT OF RAIN   36

A BOY NAMED MARCUS   38

PALE GLOW OF YOUR FLAXEN HAIR   39

WHEN CICADAS RULED THE EARTH   40

LISTEN   41

LIFE   42

YOUR STEPS ARE GOLDEN   46

EARTH IS A FRAGMENT OF SKY   48

SILENCE   49

FOR THE UNNAMED DEAD   52

THE SWEETEST SECRET   56

FIRE LAKE   59

THE THING ITSELF   62

MY FATHER'S MIND   64

REMEMBERING GEOFFREY   67

BROKEN   70

PATH

These steps of stone covered in moss
are pages of a secret text
unexpectedly unveiled
by a passing light

I can hear time
echo
between footfalls
in the stones
between breaths

The poem writes itself in the wind
lifting clouds of dust

I pause in wonder:
is my tread too heavy
are my steps too loud

HEART TEACHER

Diaphanous between worlds
prayer flags dance
awakening dormant syllables
set free by the wind

A memory resurfaces
pale gold between my eyes
like fire in water

Suddenly
universes unfold
unravelling certainties

I awaken in your dream
and find
your laughing eyes
in the backward glance
of a three-legged dog

SHUG DRAK (1)

The wind is a mantra
architect of the cave

My tears
A garland of pearls
fresh from the sea

I sit
in timeless wonder
free of ambition

Shug Drak

Shug Drak is one of the four holy cliffs of the sacred
Bumthang Valley in Bhutan. The temple at Shug Drak is said
to have been blessed by Guru Rinpoche in the 8th century and
is dedicated to him. A cave with a prayer wheel turned by
an old man leads up to the small temple where Guru Rinpoche
meditated for 2 years, leaving hand and foot prints on the
rock face.

SHUG DRAK (2)

The face of wisdom
burns brightly in this cool dark cave
A living presence
breathing in and breathing out

A prayer in stone

Nameless mantras
reverberate through time
through these walls
pervading space

I evaporate
A palpating transparency
between realities

Each blade of grass
every open flower
a mudra
catching endless drops of compassion
from your unblemished heart

DISSOLUTION

Thoughts are just shadows
fugitives of the mind
restless phantoms
with nowhere to go

Unclaimed
thoughts will exhaust themselves
self-immolate
and dissolve back into space

Then all you perceive
will appear just as it is:
insubstantial
like air

SURRENDER

Soaring like an eagle in mid-flight
the open mind
is a fearless state

Having surrendered to its own nature
the mind
becomes true again
like the eagle
lifted by the moment
free of itself

OFFERING

The water mill whispers
to the prayer wheel
sending blessings through the wind

A wild dog's bark is as sacred
as OM MANI PADME HUM

When the view is constant
there is no difference
between a handful of gold
and a handful of shit

LAMP OFFERING (for Valentina)

Cross swiftly my friend
to the other shore
Go without fear

Let the light of a thousand lamps guide you
and bless you
so that you find your way home
shedding the tender shackles
of the life you left behind

LAMA

The evening sun erases itself
undoes the shadows of the past
and illuminates the ground before me

A lama appears in the distance
then vanishes
without trace

Blue flame of day cools into night

The lama
A brief presence
held only in my mind's gaze

Lama

Lama is a title for a teacher or spiritual master of the
Dharma in Tibetan Buddhism. The title is similar to the
Sanskrit term Guru.

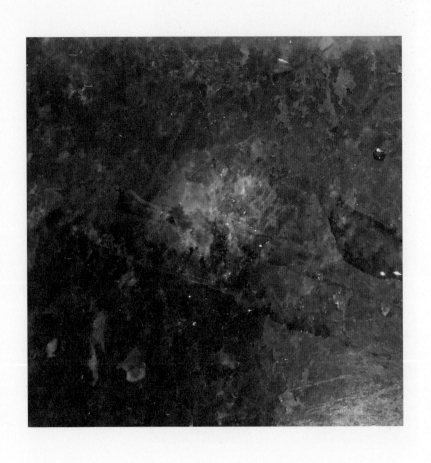

SHUG DRAK (3)

The old man
turns the prayer wheel
and chants to a forgotten rhythm
belonging to another world

My palms meet in greeting
He returns the gesture
with a toothless smile

The prayer wheel turns

The rhythm becomes an extension
of his breath
my breath

Every now and then a solitary bell

Am I dreaming I wonder
as he dissolves
into the unearthly light

LAND OF
THE THUNDER DRAGON

Stones
stained by centuries of burnt offerings
hallowed ground of ash and blood
land of shamans and myths
magicked into existence
on the length of a hermit's breath

I open my eyes
my mind a handful of dust
reborn in this strange new land

Nameless images
turn in the wind
and drown in my eyes

Drunk with love
my mind
has become one with this enchantment
naked and untamed

UNSTRUCK SOUND

Silence
unfolds into sound
Sound
unfolds into the void

Sound of the void
has neither beginning nor end
A sacred thread
running through time
into space

Each thought
Each breath
Each cell that trembles
trembles with the quiet majesty of the void

Unstruck Sound

The Vedic concept of the 'unstruck sound', Anahata Nada,
refers to 'the sound that is not made by two things striking
together'. It is the sound of primal energy, the sound of
the universe itself. The ancients say that the audible sound
which most resembles this is the syllable OM.

BLACK SKY IN SUMMER

Saturn's daughter
heavy with longing for something other

Indra waits
sword unsheathed

Black sky in summer
split asunder
by an act of compassion

The horizon opens
spilling liquid gold onto cracked earth
An embrace without shadows

Unexpected ode
disguised as an elegy

Black sky in summer
embers of a day dream
fades into a thousand shades
of light blue grey

AT THE FULL MOON

At the full moon
the sea
unbuttons her cloak of darkness
with fingers of remembering

Unfurling past into present
she shares her innermost secrets
with the unbound night
a net of jewels
cast adrift
undulating
to the rhythm
of her unbroken breath

All her treasures unveiled
a body of dreams held afloat
by night's fleeting gaze

This night she whispers
She opens her arms of water
and calls me back
to the silken folds
of her ageless womb

I DREAMT OF RAIN

Last night I dreamt of rain
pounding through a blood red sky
A *tour de force* cleansing the world
of all its stains

I dreamt of rain
profound and unrelenting
open palms of liquid crystal
drawing in a cinnabar sky

Sleeping in my chamber of rain
dreaming dreams within dreams

Ouroboros
iridescent over my crown
a blue fire
renewing
casting its spell over the obsidian night

Ouroboros

Ouroboros is an ancient symbol, first emerging in ancient
Egypt and India, depicting a serpent or dragon devouring
its own tail. It often symbolises self-reflexivity and the
cyclical nature of existence, in the sense of something
constantly re-creating itself. It can also represent the
idea of a primordial unity. The Ouroboros has often been
used in alchemical illustrations, symbolising the cyclical
nature of the alchemist's opus. Carl Jung interpreted the
Ouroboros as having archetypal significance to the human
psyche.

A BOY NAMED MARCUS

I want the night to carry me
like giant waves on the sea
to a land untold
on a cool blue breeze

Adrift on a bed of stars
I close my eyes and dream
I hear a familiar tune
faint but still sweet

Tonight
I shall don a magic cloak
play my golden flute
and weave a lullaby
with silken faerie wings

Come along and you'll see why
this place between earth and sky
is so precious to me

PALE GLOW OF
YOUR FLAXEN HAIR

I have no memory of your face
but I will always know it
iridescent
as day dreams itself into night

Winter's breath upon my cheek
Your amber gaze full with longing
Pale glow of your flaxen hair
set adrift by the waxing moon

Before I know it
I too am golden
A goddess
emerging from the dark night sky
shedding a skin of dying stars

WHEN CICADAS
RULED THE EARTH

When cicadas ruled the earth
they dined on song alone
Messengers
from a world untouched

These phantom echoes haunt us still
A link to that dimension
before language
before thought
when each perception
was a feast of sensual convergence
complete in itself

When cicadas ruled the earth
sea and sky were one
held together by a fragile skeleton of sounds

delicately balanced and finely tuned

Incomparable resonance

Unstruck sound

LISTEN

The tree remembers its beginnings
providing shade
for the earth that gave it life

When did we start forgetting
When did we stop seeing
When did we stop listening
or giving back

The all-seeing tree sits in serene repose
trusting the Earth
knowing that we are
One body   One breath   One life

LIFE

The moment we are born
death envelops us
like a second skin

Time spins its web of hope and fear
numbing senses
and coarsening desires
until one day
we find ourselves helpless
immobile
A shrivelled cocoon
waiting to burst into life

YOUR STEPS ARE GOLDEN

Your steps are golden
but the soles of your feet
are stained with blood of the earth

Your blood

A thousand cuts
Your flayed flesh
covered in ash

They say
gold has no shadow
They say one day
gold
will be flowing through your blackened veins
like fire

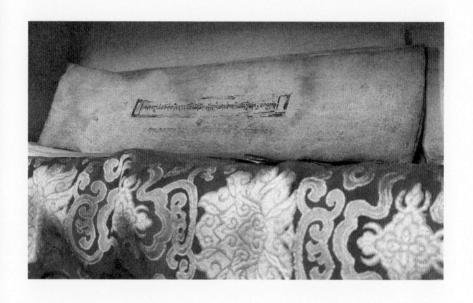

EARTH IS
A FRAGMENT OF SKY

Earth is a fragment of sky
a fallen star
pale with longing
haunted by memories of beginnings

The moon sheds tears
of forgetting and remembering
endless drops of liquid amber
cleansing wounds with the salt of time

How to forget
when you are suspended between breaths
shadowless
still unfolding each other's dreams

SILENCE

Silence spreads its arms of air
envelops everything
and retreats back into itself
a perfect cocoon of contentment

Later
it will be ruptured
undone
but that's for later
not now

FOR THE UNNAMED DEAD

Who will mourn
when all those who remember have gone
when ashes have become earth
and the earth stained with your blood
has cracked and crumbled
when your features
no longer relevant
have been undone by time

Who will hear
the hollow echoes of your cries
when tears rain red from the skies
and the seas run dry

What is left
when all the witnesses have gone

There is a part of us that never forgets
We are waves
in a single body of consciousness

The seasons bear witness
the elements bear witness
we are the same breath of life
the same life reborn

THE SWEETEST SECRET

Krishna's flute loosens its tongue
unravelling   images
that wash through me
anointing all my senses

A baptism of light

Emptied
I rise and float
towards sacred Chomolungma
ambrosia on my unsuspecting lips

Only the cascading timbre of the santoor
brings me back down
smiling

The sweetest secret
a silent tremor in my heart

Unbidden butterfly
from an enchanted land

Chomolungma

Chomolungma is the original Tibetan name for what became
popularly known in the West as Mount Everest. It means
'Goddess Mother of the World ; in Sanskrit it is known as
Sagarmatha, which means 'Ocean Mother'. It is the highest
point on the earth's surface, and is considered to be a most
sacred place.

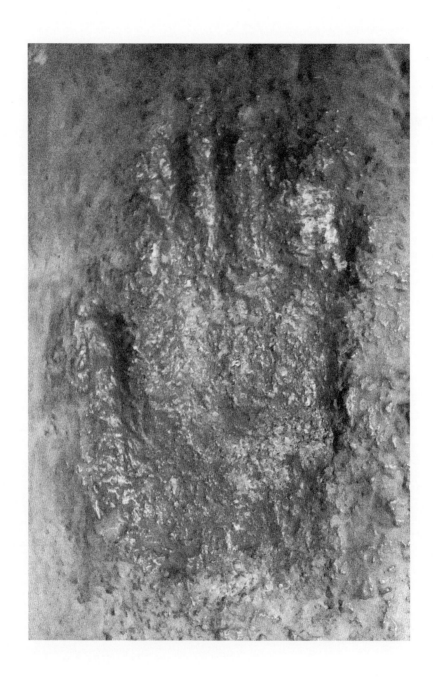

FIRE LAKE

The man unwinds his shroud and rises naked
as pale as the moon is full
a crown of disembodied dreams
discarded at his ashen feet

Eyes of mercury
iridescent
as he steps longingly
into the Lake of Fire
lost in swathes of saffron vapour

Kalpas unfold
he emerges between worlds
wearing a crown of fire
and silks of unearthly gold

Mirrored eyes seeing all
the man
vanishes into light
unwriting all the words ever written
unspeaking all the words ever spoken

Fire Lake

Legend has it that the Saint and Siddha Pema Lingpa (1450-1521), foremost of the 5 Tertön Kings (Treasure Seekers), dove into the Burning Lake (Mebar Tsho in Bumthang, Bhutan) to recover dharma treasures, a butter lamp burning brightly in one hand. He told onlookers that if he was an imposter then his lamp would be extinguished. He eventually emerged with a statue and treasure casket full of scrolls tucked under one arm, the butter lamp still burning fiercely in his hand.

Kalpa

Kalpa is a Sanskrit word meaning an aeon. According to Buddhist and Hindu cosmology, a kalpa is the period of time between the creation and recreation of a world or universe.

THE THING ITSELF

The forest empties its lungs and says
the thing itself does not exist
what seems to be a vague memory
is nothing but a rumour

The thing you are looking for
hovers between points of view
crosses the diaphanous curtain between thoughts
and becomes something other

Forms of smoke and water
begin and die in my eyes

Tonight
I am the dewdrop
I am the leaf
I am the smallest hum
carrying all the sounds of the universe

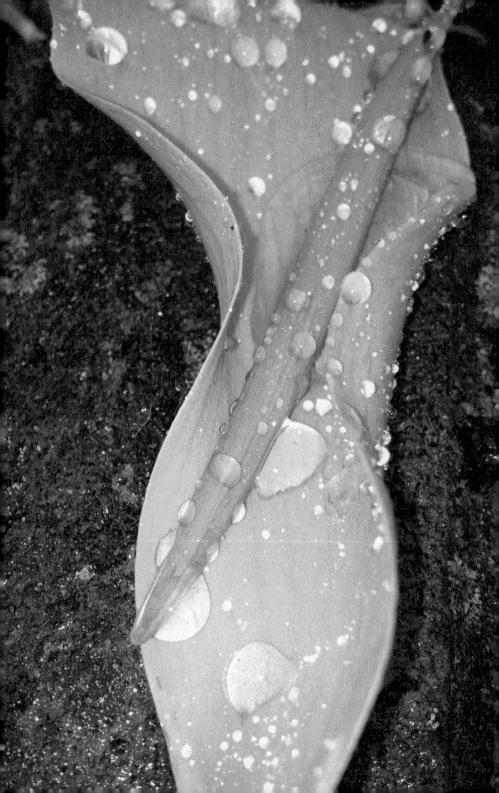

MY FATHER'S MIND

My father the poet
lived in the distant past
his memory a sacrifice
to the Gods of Time

If all memory were ritual
a labyrinth of scars
then the poet without memory
should wander free and easy
each step a budding lotus

The ruins of the poet's mind
remained a monument to the past
a crumbling edifice of shadows
suspended between forgotten syllables

REMEMBERING GEOFFREY

Come and have tea with me
You called to say
Today is Marcel Proust's birthday

It's been so long since I've seen you
Will you come for tea

Come and keep me company
let us pretend
just for a day
that I don't have HIV

Come and have tea with me today
It's Marcel Proust's birthday

BROKEN

The night was still

Lightening broke the sky

Thunder broke the silence

My heart
no longer still
broken
by the memory of you

every now
and then
a solitary bell

by Chiang Yomei

INK PUBLISHING
NO.463

Author	Chiang Yomei
Chief editor	Chu An-min
English editor	Hallie Campbell
Executive editor	Chen Chienyu
Designer	Akira Lai
Proofreader	Wu Rosa, Chiang Yomei

Publisher	Chang Shu-min
Publishing	INK Literary Monthly Publishing Ltd.
Address	8F, No.249, Jian 1st Rd., Zhonghe Dist., New Taipei City 23553, Taiwan R.O.C.
Telephone	02-22281626
Fax	02-22281598
E-mail	ink.book@msa.hinet.net
Website	http://www.sudu.cc

General agent	Rising Sun Publishing Ltd.
Telephone	03-3589000
Fax	03-3556521
Postal service	19000691 Rising Sun Publishing Ltd.
Printing	Hai Wang printing Ltd.

General agent in Hong Kong & Macau /Global China Circulation & Distribution Limited

Address   2/F, 7 Chun Cheong Street, Tseung Kwan O Industrial Estate, Hong Kong

Telephone   (852)27982220

Fax   (852)27965471

Website   www.gccd.com.hk

Publishing date   November, 2015 the first edition

PRICE   299 NTD

CIP 851.486

ISBN 978-986-387-061-6

All the proceeds of this book will be donated to the Khyentse Foundation, whose purpose is to create a system of support for the continuing study and practice of the Buddhadharma.

印刻文學 463

赤裸的心

蔣友梅

作者：蔣友梅

總 編 輯：初安民 | **責任編輯：**陳健瑜 | **美術編輯：**賴維明 | **校對：**吳美滿、陳健瑜、蔣友梅

發行人：張書銘 | **出版：**INK 印刻文學生活雜誌出版有限公司・新北市中和區建一路 249 號 8 樓 | **電話：**02-22281626 | **傳真：**02-22281598 | **E-mail：**ink.book@msa.hinet.net | **網址：**舒讀網 http://www.sudu.cc

法律顧問：巨鼎博達法律事務所・施竣中律師 | **總代理：**成陽出版股份有限公司 | **電話：**03-3589000（代表號）| **傳真：**03-3556521 | **郵政劃撥：**19000691，成陽出版股份有限公司 | **印刷：**海王印刷事業股份有限公司 | **港澳總經銷：**泛華發行代理有限公司 | **地址：**香港新界將軍澳工業邨駿昌街 7 號 2 樓 | **電話：**(852) 2798 2220 | **傳真：**(852) 2796 5471 | **網址：**www.gccd.com.hk | **出版日期：**2015 年 11 月 初版 | **ISBN**：978-986-387-061-6 | **定價：**299 元

國家圖書館出版品預行編目資料

版權所有・翻印必究

本書如有破損、缺頁或裝訂錯誤，請寄回本社更換

赤裸的心 / 蔣友梅作 . -- 初版 . -- 新北市：INK 印刻文學, 2015.11
面； 公分 . -- (印刻文學；463)
ISBN：978-986-387-061-6（精裝）　　　CIP 851.486 104018023

本書所有版稅全部捐給欽哲基金會。欽哲基金會是宗薩仁波切在 2001 年創立的非營利慈善組織。其目的在於護持佛法的傳承及研究，和幫助舉世修行者致力修持佛陀大智、大悲、大悟的教法。